Third edition published in 2025 by Rookscroft Publishing
rookscroft.com

ISBN 978-1-0684543-0-1

Written and illustrated by Jayne Siroshton.

This is a work of fiction. Any resemblance to actual persons, living or dead, is purely coincidental.

Printed in India

Books by Jayne Siroshton

All Feathers and Hats

Circus of the Crescent Moon

Into the Wild Woods

My sincerest thanks to Sarah Shafer for
taking the time to edit this little book.

and to Roshni Rajshekhar Nsir for your
lovely calligraphy.

ALL FEATHERS AND HATS

Written and Illustrated
by
Jayne Siroshton

Rookscroft House in the Autumn

THE SALISH SEA

ROOKSCROFT

THE HEDGEROWS

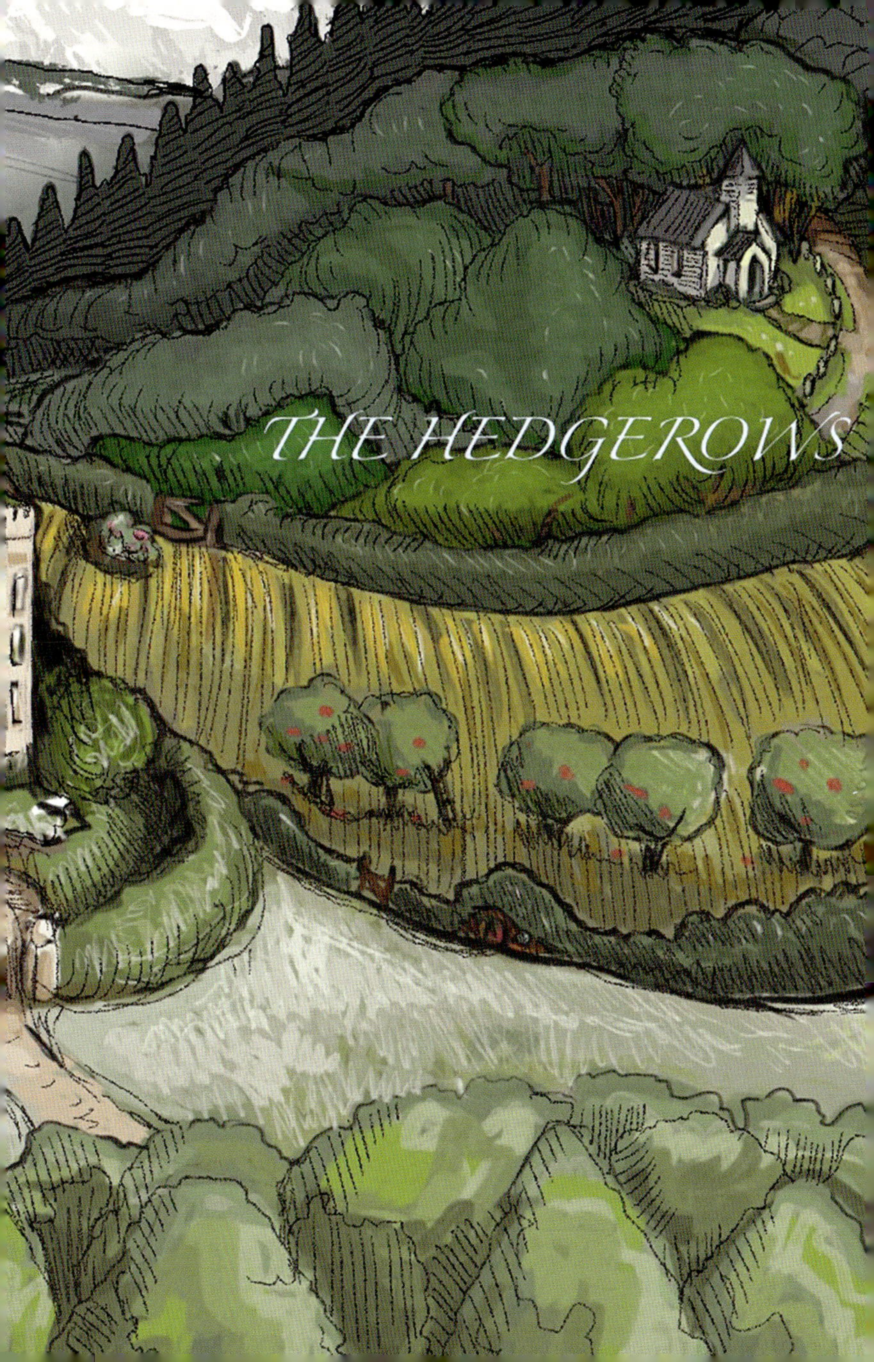

Chapter One

An Unexpected Guest

I first met Vernon on a lovely morning in late summer. I was in the study trying, unsuccessfully, to set up a still life with a handful of apples and an old chipped bowl when I happened to glance over to the large picture window that overlooks the sea, and there he was, in the lower left-hand corner, peering in.

He was a lovely-looking pheasant with beautiful plumage. Stretched up tall to see over the windowsill, he held his head to one side, he viewed the room with a round yellow eye, and on his head, he wore a tall battered top hat pulled down quite low.

"Now, who put a hat on that poor bird?" I wondered out loud, "And how on earth is it staying on?"

I watched in amusement and disbelief as he slowly

looked around the room, his head bobbing about in quick little movements until finally, he peered to the far back where I was standing, and our eyes met. I saw a flicker of recognition, and he seemed to jump slightly.

Slowly, I backed up and left the study, then made my way to the front door. I was hoping to quietly walk to the side of the house to catch another glimpse of him before he left, but I was interrupted before my first step by a loud, high cough as he cleared his throat. I looked down, and there he stood, right before me on the doormat.

He coughed again and then, to my amazement, began to speak! "I would like to take this opportunity to introduce myself. I am your neighbour. My name is Vernon Cotterill. Most Noble Vernon Cotterill, the third, to be exact. I believe my ancestral roots stem from the Normans, and it goes without saying that I am an honourable gentleman, very well known in these parts. I am here to inquire about your skills in portraiture."

I could barely take in his words, for the shock of seeing his small yellow beak opening and closing at every word and the odd jerky movement of his head as he spoke was almost too much to bear. His voice was confident yet scratchy, and when he had said his piece, he looked me directly in the eye, waiting for my response. My first impulse, I am ashamed to admit, was to giggle. My second (hardly much better) was to bend down and scoop him up as I had done so many times with my pet birds, but clearly, this would be the wrong thing to do. So I invited him in for some tea and a chat, an offer which he accepted.

He drank Earl Grey, "the tea of nobility," as he called it, black and weak from the cup that I placed on the table before him. There was a slight faux pas with the biscuits; I offered them whole and dry, to which he looked askance before informing me that when entertaining birds of a certain social set, it is customary to offer a biscuit pre-soaked in a little tea on a plate or shallow saucer so it could be eaten without incident.

"Where do you paint?" asked Vernon after taking a few tentative sips.

"I have a little studio through that door," I gestured. "Would you like me to show you 'round?"

"Perhaps..." he paused to drink a little tea, "That is if I decide to have my portrait painted."

"I would love to paint you!" I gushed enthusiastically. "You are quite unique! I must admit, I have no experience with painting birds, but I think I could get the hang of the feathers if I practise."

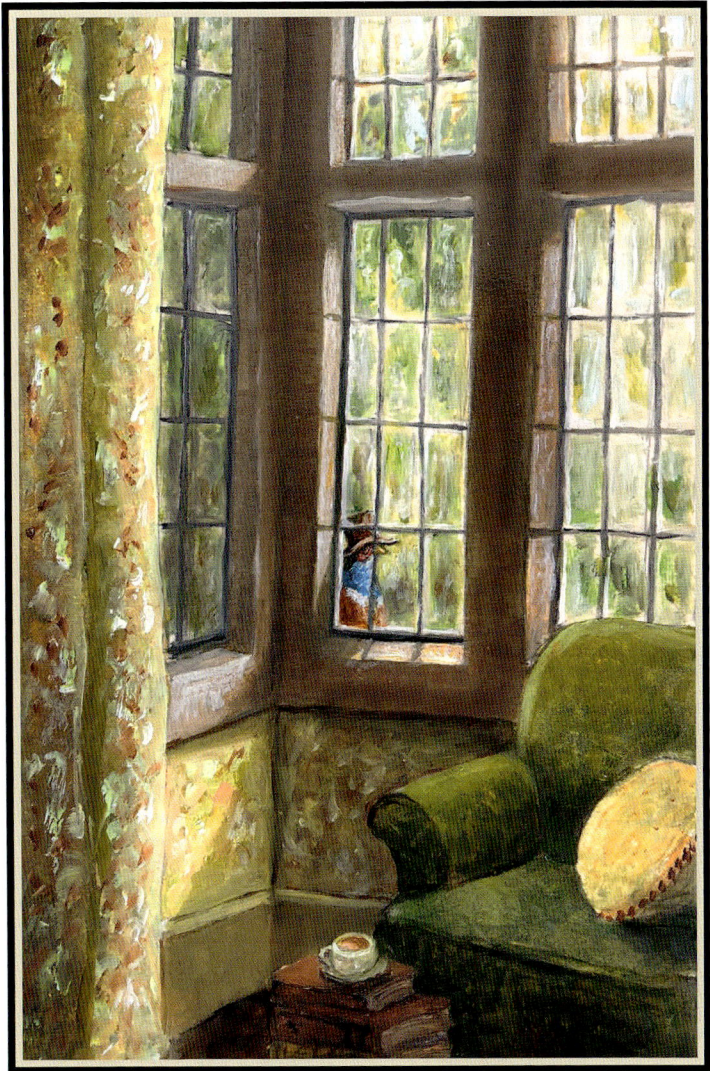

Vernon Peeking in Through the Window

He was not impressed and turned his head to look at me full-on with his left eye. "I do not wish to sound rude," he responded, "But I am hardly the sitter to practise on. Do you have classical training of some kind? Are you a noted artist or important in some way?"

"No, not at all," I replied, smiling. "I simply enjoy painting, and as I like to paint and you would like to be painted, I suggest we give it a go! After all, there is nothing to lose. You are such a handsome pheasant. I would love to paint you." The last comment seemed to do the trick. I was dying to paint him sitting there all proud and strange, with his odd, weathered hat and spectacular plumage.

He paused, thinking for a moment, "I have often been referred to as handsome, sometimes striking, and I understand your desire to paint me, of course. I suppose sitting for a portrait might not be an unpleasant experience, all things considered..."

"There will be biscuits and tea," I promised.

Vernon

"Very good," he replied a little condescendingly. "Yes, I imagine I can do that. If it is a good likeness, it can go on display. If not, it will need to be burned." This seemed a little extreme, but I held my tongue, and he continued. "It will need to capture my noble bearing, my status, the exquisite iridescence of my neck feathers. A picture of me in my finest hour. The Church on Foxes Lane has a meeting room, and they are lining the hallway with paintings of local dignitaries. I have been invited to submit a portrait, and, well, there is a certain lady..." Vernon lowered his eyes and gazed into his tea, "When I see her, I feel, I mean, I don't feel, well...quite as composed as I might. I think that perhaps, perhaps if she saw me at my best, in a grand painting" and at this, his voice trailed off.

For the briefest moment right then, when I looked at him, and he glanced up, his confident outer shell had fallen away, and in his eyes, I could clearly see a sensitive soul. He read my thoughts and blinked heavily, shook his head (his hat stayed right in place), and when he looked back, and his eyes had reopened, they had resumed the look of beady indifference. But I had seen him. I had seen him as he truly was, and that was just how I intended to paint him.

Sometime later, after I had shown him around my studio, we stood by the door as he prepared to leave. "Well," said Vernon, "It has been very pleasant getting to know you. I am sure you are eager to get started on my portrait, but as you can understand, I am very busy. I am a prominent businessman. As you probably know."

"How fabulous! I had no idea! Did you make the hat you are wearing today?" I replied, gesturing towards the top of his head.

"Oh, that one, yes, it's rather a trademark of mine. A bit banged up, but it has character. As I was saying, I am very busy, and my time is limited, so we will need to make an appointment."

"Yes, absolutely! I'm mostly here pottering about the house. Just let me know when you have time, and we can set a date."

"Well, let me see. Tomorrow morning, I am free at ten sharp."

"Same time tomorrow, that will be perfect," I replied with a smile.

He nodded, bowed slightly, turned on his heel, and was off.

Front Door

Chapter Two

The Sketch

I woke early the next morning, curious and eager to get to work. I tidied my studio, cleaned the palette, and squeezed out some oils for the underpainting. At nine forty-five, I put on the kettle and laid a shortcake biscuit in a shallow bone china saucer, ready for the tea.

Having no idea of Vernon's punctuality, I tried to stay near the door, waiting for a knock. By five past ten, I thought he was being fashionably late, and my opinion of him began to falter. By ten-fifteen, I had given up on him and was making my way back to the kitchen through the hallway when I heard a soft pecking at the front door, and I opened it to find a rather disgruntled pheasant who shot me a withering glance. A bag was slung over his left wing, and his hat tipped slightly to one side, obscuring an eye.

"Well, hello," I said cheerily. "I am sorry I didn't hear you. Have you been waiting long?"

"I have been here for some considerable time, but my knocking went unanswered." He replied dramatically, "I strongly suggest you invest in a second doorbell set lower down for visitors of a more..." he coughed slightly, "diminutive stature."

"Wonderful idea!" I agreed, ushering him inside. "I am sorry I didn't hear you, Vernon. Please come in and have some tea."

In the studio, he took a great interest in the palette that I had selected, feeling it was flat and would not do him justice. I explained that it was simply intended for the underpainting and the more vivid colours would be added later. I began to explain my painting technique, but glancing over realised I had totally lost him, so I suggested he make himself comfortable while I went to fetch the tea.

Upon returning, I was shocked to see he had switched his battered hat for a rigid bowler, which was frankly too small and perched precariously on top of his head. I hope he never reads this (but fear he will and will rightly be offended), but he looked a little absurd sitting there so stiffly.

I set the tray on the table. "Vernon," I ventured, trying

to repress a giggle, "the new hat is very fine, but I so prefer you in the hat you arrived in. It suits you so well."

He was obviously hurt and did not move or speak for several seconds while formulating his scathing reply.

"Dearest Jayne," he sighed, as though addressing a small child, "I don't expect you to understand the upper classes, but this hat is far more fitting to my status and place in society than the one I walked in wearing. Now, please proceed with the underpainting." And with that, he resumed his stiff posture and prepared to be painted.

I collected my thoughts before replying. I had set my mind on capturing him as I had seen him the day before, an authentic painting of his real self, so I had to think quickly.

"I am sorry, Vernon. I had no idea you were one of those creatures who follow the fashions of the day," I said, "Of course, keep your hat on if that is how you wish to be portrayed. Now I just have to pop back to the kitchen to fetch our biscuits, if you will excuse me..." and with that, I turned to leave.

Vernon in an Unfortunate Hat Choice

When I returned, I was relieved to see that Vernon had switched back to his original hat, though it was a little askew, and was pacing the room in an unsettled manner.

"Do you think this hat gives me a sufficiently debonair air?" He asked as I set his biscuit plate on the table.

"Why yes!" I replied enthusiastically. "It's a little rakish. I think your lady friend will like it. It adds a little mystery."

He visibly flinched at my comment, and I instantly regretted making it. "I'm sorry, I didn't mean to..." I began.

"No need for apologies," he snapped. "Let's just get on with the portrait, shall we? I haven't got all day." His eyes darted around the room, "I am unfamiliar with the process. Shall we pack a picnic and head out to the fields?"

"Um, no, I think the studio is better for today," I replied.

"Please stand over by the window. I think that is just the right sort of light."

"Surely you don't intend to paint me back here with nothing but that old wallpaper and faded curtain as a backdrop?" he cried aghast. "This painting is not at all how I imagined at all!"

"Oh, don't worry," I soothed. "I'll paint you first, then add a lovely background later; what scene were you thinking?"

"I have decided on the wheat field." He replied.

"Would you mind straightening your hat?" I asked (since he had changed hats while I was out of the room, I was curious to see how he managed such a feat). Slowly, he shifted his weight and effortlessly brought his right foot up as he lowered his head to meet it. Then, with one fluid movement, he grasped the brim of the hat with his toes and expertly adjusted the angle before re-assuming his original posture. It was very impressive.

I picked up my brush and began to sketch. "Once I get a rough outline going, you're welcome to relax," I told him, but he stared fixed, straight ahead and did not speak.

As I painted, a deep calm filled the room, and the painting came easily. Vernon was a handsome bird and remarkably easy to capture, so I had the gist of him down quite quickly.

"Really, Vernon, you're welcome to move around now. I think I have the lines in," I said. He blinked slowly but remained stiff and still.

"How long have you been making hats?" I asked, eager to help him relax.

"Since I was a chick," he replied. "I am rather well known for my millinery. I make hats for all sorts of clients."

The thought crossed my mind that perhaps other creatures wore hats too, and maybe they also spoke, an idea that was very exciting. "Who do you make them for?" I asked excitedly.

"Anyone who wants them, rabbits, foxes, badgers...I have numerous customers," he replied.

Silence fell upon the room once more, and my mind whirled with visions of creatures the likes of which I had never imagined before. I so wanted to know more about them all but tried my best to suppress my excitement.

"Please tell me, how did you come to have such an interesting occupation?" I asked.

"I fell into it," he replied coolly.

"Is that common?" I continued, trying to draw him out.

"No, I don't believe it is." He shook his head and seemed to loosen slightly. "But then, I have always been special. I have the rare gift of design and a steady beak, so my stitching is barely visible."

"How did it come about? The hat-making, I mean. Did you apprentice with a hatter, or is it a family thing?"

"It is a long story and not as fascinating as my other exploits. I have always made and worn them; friends and neighbours saw them and wanted them, too. I suppose I just fell into it." He seemed bored with my questions, almost nonchalant, but I persisted.

"Tell me about your customers, how many of them are there?" I asked.

"Too many to count." He paused and yawned slightly.

"There are quite a few around and about, in the fields and hedgerows, the copse and Wild Woods... which, by the way, is no place for a bird."

"Tell me about the Wild Woods. They sound very exciting."

"Exciting is hardly the word. They are filled with all the wrong sort of animals, lots of night dwellers...teeth... singing...that kind of thing." His eyes sharpened, and his voice became stern. "Now, enough of this nonsense, and don't stray in those woods!"

I wanted to know more, but Vernon had put an end to the conversation. The room fell silent as I resumed my painting and a deep stillness settled over my mind. I found myself humming a quiet tune of satisfaction and pleasure as my work progressed. After some time, I felt that the underpainting might finally be done. As I stood back to take a better look, I felt a little flutter of pride as the emerging picture embodied the spirit of him that I had hoped to capture in the beginning.

Sensing I was done for the day, Vernon walked stiffly over and stood by my side, considering the picture. "Not a bad start," he conceded after several minutes of careful inspection. "It needs work, but it's not without promise."

"Thank you," I replied smiling, "I don't want to keep you from your busy day," and together we made our way to the front door where he informed me that he would be returning the following morning for another sitting. Then he left, striding quickly off into the field of ripening wheat, and in moments, he was gone from view.

Vernon Walking Off Into the Wheat

Chapter Three

Feathers And Paint

Vernon visited daily, and little by little, the sepia-toned underpainting was replaced by a vibrant new image. Gradually, thin washes of reds, blues, and yellows were added to the muddy brown. It was a difficult business, and almost as much paint was removed by a rag as applied by the brush.

I worked for days on his hooded yellow eyes, trying to add colour and detail while preserving the spirit I had so spontaneously captured at the start.

As I painted, I found myself in a never-ending balancing act between saying too little and swamping my previous work with too much paint. There were moments of pride and hours of self-doubt, and I learned that painting a portrait was a far cry from the apples and flowers I had contented myself with before, especially with such a demanding and outspoken sitter.

Nonetheless, each morning, I found myself eagerly awaiting Vernon's visits, heralded by the crisp high ring of the little doorbell I had installed just for him. Often, as I painted, the conversation would turn to the comings and goings of the creatures who comprised his clientele. Either by design or lack of interest, Vernon avoided specifics, so although I had a tantalising glimpse of the magical world that ran parallel to mine it remained frustratingly out of view.

Then one day, as I was painting the details of his beak, Vernon yawned and said, "I must be going soon, I have a lot to do... the Turkey Sisters are visiting today. They are having hats made for an event," and my heart almost jumped from my chest at his casual revelation.

"Turkey sisters? Do they live nearby?" I asked excitedly.

"They live on the edge of the fields." He walked over to the window and I followed, "Just over that hill," he indicated with a gesture of his wing. "In a little old church, they hold services there."

"A church?" I stammered, as questions began to flood my mind. "Can anyone go? What are they like? Do they read from a big book? Is it well attended?"

Vernon studied me quizzically before responding in a cautious and slightly patronising tone. "Well, they have an old opossum as the pastor," He said. "He's not from round here but I think they chose him because he can read and has a very deep baritone voice, though, if he gets too worked up on a passage he can cause a bit of a scene."

It all sounded odd and wonderful, and I just had to see it for myself. "When are these services?" I asked.

"Often on Tuesdays and Thursdays," he replied matter-of-factly, "sometimes in the mornings if the weather is good. Any day if there are nice flowers to display and sometimes at dusk if there are new candles."

Vernon came over and inspected the portrait. "Yes, it's coming along," he said matter-of-factly, almost to himself, then turned toward the door.

"I don't want to keep you." I said, "Please, let me show you out." We walked together to the steps, where I wished him a lovely afternoon, and he departed.

When he returned the following day, he had a far-off look in his normally sharp eye, and I could tell that something was on his mind.

"Can it be possible to be loved if you have a flaw?" He asked suddenly.

We were sitting in the studio and he was sipping on his tea while I worked at the easel, trying to layer up the paint to indicate the soft volume of his feathers. The room was cosy and a warm breeze lazily stroked the curtains and filled the room with the promise of a perfect summer's day.

Vernon's question caught me off guard. He seemed strangely vulnerable today. "We all have flaws, Vernon," I replied, "And I hope we are still lovable."

"...Or a secret?" he continued without acknowledging my reply.

"We all have these, too, to a degree," I said.

"In my experience, it is possible to be loved only in the absence of flaws, and secrets are inevitable." He answered thoughtfully.

"I don't agree," I replied. "Beauty is in the eye of the beholder; it is our uniqueness that makes us lovable, and secrets should not exist in love."

"I am afraid I can never, never reveal my true self to someone so perfect as she..." he trailed off, lost in private thought, and his head fell slightly to the side as he looked toward the floor.

"Vernon, we all have our flaws. This girl you like, she

has them too."

His head jerked up, and he looked me in the eye. "Firstly. She is not a girl, and secondly, she is perfect in every way!" he snapped.

There was no point in contradicting him, so I nodded and stayed silent, and nothing more was said.

Vernon visited almost every day, and as the portrait developed, so did our friendship, and I found myself saddened at the thought he would soon be gone. Often, he would rush off to see his clients when we were done, and I came to know the days when he would visit the sisters by the twinkle in his eye and his light step as he ran off into the fields. I realised, with warm amusement, that one of them must be the object of his affections, though I could not tell which one.

On the final day of painting, Vernon sat beside me as I added the last details to complete the picture. I was mixing some cobalt blue with a touch of lead white to paint accents on his iridescent feathers when I suddenly felt the end was near, and a flush of sadness washed over me.

"Vernon, I think we're almost done." I said, "The wheat will be ready in a few days, and I'll sit out in the fields with your portrait and paint it in. It's just so beautiful at this time of year, and I was wondering if you have any friends who might like to be painted there too?"

"I can't say I am too fond of sharing my background with just anybody," he said, "but I have told the sisters about your skills, and they have requested to be painted wearing their new hats. I wouldn't mind sharing my background with them. If you would like to paint them, maybe you could have my finished likeness on your easel when they visit so that they can see your abilities for themselves?"

"Do you think they would come?" I asked, "I would love to paint them! Please invite them for me."

"Me invite them? Oh no, that would be socially incorrect!" Replied Vernon, "I could, however, take an invitation to them from you in the form of a note."

"Oh, would you? Thank you!" This was all very exciting.

"I am still waiting to receive some last-minute items to complete their hats. If they agree to sit for you, perhaps I could have them sent over once they are ready," he suggested.

"Absolutely, that is a wonderful idea! I really hope they accept. What are they like?" I asked.

"I hesitate to give you a description as I am not

talented in that way, but I will try. Madge is tall and proud. She has a long neck, keen eye, and talks with an air of confidence that comes with good breeding. Connie is smaller, slightly plumper, soft-eyed, quietly spoken..." He trailed off, lost in imaginings, though I could not tell which of the two had caught his fancy.

I wrote a quick note to the sisters on a card inviting them to the house while Vernon watched over me. "A lot can be discerned about a person by the quality and line of their writing," he remarked disapprovingly, and I smiled to myself. I was going to miss his visits.

He tucked the note under his wing, and we walked to the door to say our final farewells. Outside, the flowers were in full bloom, foxgloves danced under the spreading limbs of an ancient oak, and the late morning sun, filtered through high clouds, seemed warm and kind. It was a day for exploration.

"Well, I suppose this is goodbye for now," I said, crouching down to look him in the eye. "I'm sorry this is over. I've really enjoyed our time together. If you call back in a week or so, the background will be finished and dry. Would you mind pointing out the direction of the church you mentioned? I am dying to get out and explore."

"The church, well, yes," he looked far off at the top of the hill and pointed with his wing. "See the top of the tree over there?"

I looked up to where he indicated and nodded.

"Well, walk through the wheat field to that spot, and you will find a gate in the hedge. On the other side is a path that goes left down into the Wild Woods and right up through a copse of alders and over the hill. Follow the path to the right, and it will lead you to the church."

"Thank you, Vernon, take care," I said and, without thinking, leaned forward and scooped him up in a loving hug. If he was offended, he did not show it, and when I put him down, he shook out his feathers from beak to tail, bowed deeply, turned, and walked off toward the field.

"Don't forget to give the turkey sisters my note!" I called after him.

"I feel confident you will meet them soon!" He called back before vanishing into the wheat.

View of the House From the Lane Above

Vernon

Chapter Four

Others

The following morning, the weather was lovely and warm, with skimming clouds that sent shadows racing across the golden fields. I grabbed my sketchbook and pencil, closed the kitchen door, and set off toward the hedgerow at the top of the field. I found the gate that Vernon had spoken of, tucked between the trunks of two large trees, and passed through it onto the lane.

To my left, it wound downhill and disappeared into the thick, dark forest that I knew to be the Wild Woods, and to my right, it led up toward a woodland of graceful silver-barked alders that shimmered in the morning sun. I turned left and took the path uphill toward the church, but as I climbed higher, the trees began to close in, and an uncomfortable feeling played around the edges of my mind. It seemed that I was a long way from home now, and suddenly felt very alone. I was thinking I had gone too far, surely it was lunchtime, and I was about to turn around when I realised that the brow of the hill was right before me, and I continued on.

Slowly, step by step, an incredible vista came into view, rolling foothills swathed in deep green forest, snow-covered mountains, and, far below, a wide silver ribbon of river that ran to the sea. My step quickened as I began to descend, and after a few minutes, the trees on the left receded from the path, forming the backdrop to a grassy meadow edged with a white picket fence and gate. Set back and framed by large pine trees was a perfect little white clapboard church with a bell tower and double doors, the whole structure no bigger than a garden shed.

At the front, gathered on the church steps, stood an assortment of nicely dressed creatures, milling around and chatting together. I stood a little way back so as not to frighten them and watched. They were mostly birds, but also a raccoon family with several young unruly children, several rabbits, an elderly porcupine in an old hat and woollen jacket, and a fox who stood quietly to one side. Never in my wildest dreams could I have imagined a scene such as this might exist outside of a children's book, yet here it was right before me, plain as day.

A bell chimed inside the little tower, the doors were opened by unseen hands, and the animals formed an orderly line and filed in one by one, with the doors closing softly behind them.

I gingerly walked through the gate and up to a small stained glass window at the side of the door, and I was leaning forward to take a peek inside when a noise below me made me jump.

"I think you are about to tread on my foot!" I looked down and saw that the soft, languid voice belonged to a spectacular golden pheasant who was sitting under the bush below the window.

"Oh, I am sorry," I gasped. "I just thought I would take a peek inside."

"You should go in," the pheasant responded. "You'll get a better view." He quickly looked me over with his round yellow eyes, but I could not read his expression.

"Would you care to join me?" I asked. "I'm new here and a little different."

"We are all a little different," answered the pheasant with a sigh, "I am a writer and writers must be different."

At the Church Door

"A writer, oh my goodness, that sounds so interesting!" I replied enthusiastically, "What do you write?"

"Whatever I fancy," the pheasant replied vaguely. "I'm Quentin, by the way... I write poetry generally. Often under rose bushes, this one's nice and thick; it provides good shelter from the spring rains, but the comings and goings of the church frankly limit its appeal."

"I'd love to read your poetry sometime," I said and gestured to the open door. "Would you care to accompany me in?"

"For you, I will," he replied kindly, hopping up from under the bush, and together we ascended the church steps and gingerly opened the door.

Inside, the service was in full swing. Quentin and I took a seat in a pew near the back of the tiny room. At the front was a podium decorated with a swag of flowers, and there, leaning forward, was a large opossum presiding over an even larger book.

Reading From the Great Book

"I will start today's service," he said in a low rasping voice, "by reading a passage from the great book." He paused to heave open the tome to a seemingly random page before commencing. "Kingdom Animalia, phylum Chordata, class Aves, order Strigiformes, family Strigidae, genus Bubo, species Bubo virginianus. Found from the Arctic tundra to the tropical rainforest, from the desert to suburban back gardens, the Great Horned Owl is one of the most widespread and common owls in..." The possum's voice trailed off, and his eyes turned glassy.

"We're losing him again!" someone called out from the front pew.

"He's going to go!" cried out another. At that moment, he keeled back, rigid, and fell, rolling down the podium steps and came to rest on the floor, his short arms and legs sticking straight up in the air.

There was a flurry of activity in the dimly lit church, and I spotted two finely dressed turkeys rush up to give him aid. He seemed to stir a little, and between them, they helped him to his feet and sat him on a chair on the front row.

"He'll be fine!" the larger one called out confidently. "Now on with the show!"

Opossum on the Floor

Were these the turkey sisters? I watched in fascination as they fussed over the opossum for several minutes before turning and walking together behind the back of the podium and out of sight.

The band struck up, and a choir of assorted animals began to sing as an old basket was passed along the rows. It looked like a collection plate, but as it approached, I noticed that as well as putting things in, creatures were also sorting through and taking things out. When it finally reached us, I peeked inside, and in the gloomy bottom was an assortment of discarded items such as you might find at the back of a kitchen drawer. I added a button from my coat pocket and passed it to Quentin, who added a feather from his neck and removed an infeasibly short pencil, which he slipped into the bag he was carrying. The basket finally ended up on the lap of the now fully recovered opossum, who ceremonially picked it up and brought it back to the podium, where he seemed to rifle through it himself before looking up to address the crowd.

"This concludes today's service. Thank you for watching!" he muttered faintly, and with that, the congregation stood and applauded. There was a general fussing about as they collected their belongings, then, as one, inched their way towards the door and out into the late morning sun.

Quentin and I stayed until the church was almost

empty, I wanted to get another look at the sisters, but they seemed to have departed by some alternate route. Finally, once the church was empty, we left together and walked down the steps in the awkward way people do when they are unsure where the end of a conversation lies.

"Well," I said at the gate, "I suppose it's time for me to go home. Where are you off to Quentin?"

"I was thinking of going back to my favourite bush," he replied. "It's an old rambling rose in the field next to the gate that belongs to an old house back over the hill. Back in the day, they used to call it Rookscroft."

"Well, that's where I live!" I cried with great excitement. "Shall we walk back together?" He nodded, and the two of us set off, back up the sandy lane towards home.

At the top of the hill, we paused and stood to take in the view. Down past the fields flanked with dark green forest, Rookscroft sat nestled unseen except for its chimneys and further on, beyond the cliffs and sandy grasses spread a vast expanse of twinkling ocean dotted with unnamed islands. It was spectacular.

After a while, I looked down at Quentin and noticed that he carried a bag over his shoulder that seemed to hold something square and quite heavy, and I asked him what it was.

"It's my poetry book and a pen," he answered excitedly. "I've just received my very first commission!" he paused (I believe) for dramatic effect, before continuing, "It came to me in the form of a letter requesting I write a love poem to a certain lady. Would you like me to read it to you?" And without waiting for a reply, he pulled the letter from his bag, shook it open with a flourish, and began to read.

"Dear Quentin, I have heard many glowing recommendations regarding your prose, and I was hoping you might be persuaded to write a poem for me. I have met a certain lady recently who has taken my fancy, nay my heart itself.

She is quite the creature, bold and sharp with a magnificent bearing. Her sister, Connie, is a sweet creature, but I must confess that it is Madge that my heart pines for. I do not know if you are acquainted with the two of them at all, but if there is even the slightest chance that she might take an interest in such an old bird as myself, I would be over the moon with joy.

Please go ahead and write a poem to her and include these words that I feel best describe her: strong, principled, knows her own mind, sharp." Quentin's voice trailed off.

"What's wrong?" I asked.

"Well," Quentin beckoned me closer and continued in a confidential tone. "Frankly, I am having some difficulty arranging a love poem to such a character as he describes... I mean to say, well, I don't think suitors are exactly lining up for this one."

"There is someone for everyone," I replied, stifling a giggle. "What's he like?"

"His name is Dr Grenville Postlethwaite," replied Quentin. "I hesitate to use the word bumbling, but there, I just did. He is a kindly old heron. Stalking, severe looking, but really a vanilla ice cream of a man... slightly melted."

"He sounds nice," I replied with sincere amusement. We began walking again. The path seemed much friendlier with Quentin by my side, and we ambled along in comfortable silence for some time until we came to the gate. Passing through, I instantly spotted a magnificent rose bush heavy with soft pink blooms. "Welcome to my home," said Quentin, gesturing with his wing. "Would you care to stay awhile?" and with that, he flopped down on the soft grass. I nodded and sat beside him, warm in the afternoon sun.

Bees drifted drunkenly from flower to flower in the rose-scented air serenaded by the chirping of crickets from the field. Quentin leaned to one side and began to softly flick fine dust onto his feathers with his left foot.

"I hope you don't mind me performing my ablutions next to you like this, but the cool earth feels lovely," he said. I smiled in reply and listened to the rhythmic scratching of the dry ground and the soft rustle of his feathers as my mind drifted away.

"What's in your bag?" he asked.

"Oh, this?" I held up my satchel and opened the flap. "It's my sketchbook and pencils. I love to draw."

"An artist, I knew it!" he replied.

"Oh, I don't know if you would call me that exactly." I laughed. "I do my best to practise every day."

"Well, you can practise on me," replied Quentin, sitting up slightly.

"I would love to, if you don't mind," I answered, taking out my pencils.

"If I minded, I wouldn't have offered." He adjusted his posture and looked directly into my eyes. "Please proceed."

I opened my book and began to sketch, starting with

his beak. "I loved seeing the church today," I began. "All those fascinating creatures. I think I even caught a glimpse of the turkey sisters."

"Madge and Connie? You know them?" he asked, barely moving.

"Not personally, but I have spent some time with Vernon Cotterill recently, painting his picture. Do you know him? The fellow who makes hats..."

"Know him? Yes," he replied without seeming to open his beak. "I know him quite well, he made this for me," he gestured upward with his eyes toward his hat.

"Do you know much about the sisters?" I asked. "I get the feeling he has his eye on one of them."

"Does he indeed?" Quentin spoke again without seeming to move. "Well, I hope for his sake it's Connie. She is a sweet, if simple, bird; she sews, arranges flowers, cooks well, keeps a nice tidy house--has absolutely NO vices!" (He said this as though it might not be a virtue.) "The girl is as pure as the driven snow... Oh, and as cute as a button."

"She sounds perfect for him, being the upstanding creature he is. And Madge?"

"Oh goodness, Jayne. Remember the letter? Strong,

principled... what was it again... sharp? And that was a description from old Postlethwaite, her suitor! ...a fellow who is speaking of her in the most glowing of terms!" Though his head had not moved, his eyes were glowing with mirth. He leaned forward, and his voice dropped to a whisper, "Believe me when I tell you, she is more than a bit of a handful, not many would be up to the task."

I tried not to laugh, but could not help myself. "If what you say is true, let's hope it's Connie who has caught his eye. I believe they will be visiting me soon to have their portraits painted."

"I don't envy you that," Quentin replied impishly.

He reassumed his former posture and I continued to sketch him, trying to capture his soft and languid beauty. His eyes were perfectly round like the little glass ones made for a toy; there was such an innocence about him... though his tongue could be quite cutting in its honesty.

We sat in this way for a long time, until the sun began to fade to the west and it felt like supper. I invited him home, but he declined, saying he had a sandwich and he was looking forward to finishing it off. So we parted ways for the evening and I promised to visit him the very next day.

Quentin

Chapter Five

Connie

The following morning, after I had completed my chores, I put together a little picnic to share with Quentin, packed up my paint supplies, and set off up the hill. The weather was lovely and the golden glow of the late summer sun set the wheat field ablaze in a glorious light.

As I approached the top of the hill, I saw a large brown bird bending over, quite absorbed in some task, and as I drew closer, I saw that she was a turkey who wore a green paisley shawl over her shoulders. I hoped she might be one of the sisters. I got quite close, and she didn't seem to notice me but stood quite still, looking down at the path. As I reached her, I followed her gaze and saw a pretty embroidered handkerchief lying on the ground.

"Would you like me to help you pick that up?" I asked.

She jumped a little at my voice and answered without looking up, "Oh no, thank you, I put it there on purpose."

Looking closely, I saw a small brown moth climbing onto the handkerchief. Once he had accomplished the task, he paused momentarily then fluttered his wings.

"I saw him on the road," said the sister, " and I'm so glad I did not step on him! I think he needs help drying out so he can fly away."

"That's very kind of you...er..."

"Connie, my name is Connie," she replied, glancing up shyly. "We all deserve a little kindness, don't we?" She was pretty, and her sweet green eyes were slightly wrinkled at the outer corners as though she were smiling.

"Hello, Connie, I'm Jayne," I replied. "I live down the hill in the Rookscroft house. I hear you might visit me soon to have your portrait painted. I hope you do. I'm looking forward to spending time with you and your sister."

Connie and the Handkerchief

"Oh yes," she replied in her gentle, quiet voice. "Hello, Jayne. We are hoping to call on you sometime early next week if that is convenient. We are both overjoyed at the thought of a painting. I never even dreamed anything like this could happen, Vernon tells us you are very skilled."

"I'll do my best and you are welcome to visit anytime, Connie. I look forward to seeing you soon."

"We do, too," she replied. "I hope you enjoy the rest of your day; the weather is lovely," and with that, she resumed her watch over the little moth while he dried out in the morning sun.

I soon reached Quentin's rose bush and found him in his leafy home, towards the back, taking a dust bath.

"Good morning!" I called out. He sat up, shook out his feathers, and picked his way toward me over the thorny branches.

"Hello," he replied in his soft, scratchy voice. "I was just getting prettied up for you."

"I've brought my paints today and a little breakfast if you're hungry." (He seemed a little absent-minded, and I was not sure if he had remembered to eat.)

"Yes, I am a little...if you can spare a crumb..." he replied.

I laid out the blanket, opened my basket, and took out a wedge of cut-and-come-again cake, which he seemed very excited to see. He came over, sat on the blanket, and eyed the cake with excitement. I sat down next to him, then set up my little easel and arranged some paints on the palate.

"There's no need to pose yet," I reassured him. "Please relax and enjoy the cake. I can work from the sketch I made of you last time."

Quentin ate his cake with great enthusiasm. "I love the currants," he commented between bites, "they add a nice chew."

"So tell me a little about yourself," I began after he had taken a few pecks, "why do you choose to live under this bush? And where is the rest of your family?"

In my mind, I had decided that he did not quite seem fully grown, and I was beginning to worry about his welfare. I had been raised to think that artists and writers, though wonderful in their own way, did not somehow have a firm grasp on the realities of living, and he seemed to be cast in that mould.

"I like the smell of the roses," he replied, "it helps create the right atmosphere for my work, and the thorns protect me from less gracious neighbours. I dread the thought of becoming dinner."

"How do you stay dry when the weather turns?" I asked.

"I haven't really thought that far ahead," he replied. "I prefer to live moment to moment."

I took out a flask and poured us some tea. "Where is your family, Quentin?" I asked again. "Do you have friends nearby?"

"My family are all long gone..." he dismissed airily, "an ill-advised day trip down to the bay, not one of them ever returned..."

"I am so sorry!" I gasped, "That's terrible."

"Don't be, you didn't do it," he waved his wing towards the North as he elaborated, "the path they took goes through the Wild Woods-not a place for ground birds-besides, they are in a better place, and someday I will join them again. I see them in the shifting clouds." He paused and gazed at the clear blue sky, "I sense them all around me."

I was curious to know how many had gone on that fateful day trip but decided to let the matter lie. As we sat quietly together, I wondered how alone he might be. "So, how about friends? You seem to know Vernon quite well. Who else is here?"

"We field creatures are all friends and acquaintances, though I tend to know more about people than know people. I always feel a little, well, on the edge of things, I suppose. As though I really don't quite belong. Everyone seems to be in such a hurry, moving too fast and thinking too much to enjoy the day. I find the whole thing very tiring."

"I understand," I agreed, "but don't you feel lonely? Wouldn't you like more intimate company?"

"Company of any sort comes at a price," Quentin replied. He had eaten the cake and was now leisurely chewing on the end of a grass stalk. "You have to be careful who you converse with, I find the less that's said, the better, generally speaking." He paused to scratch his neck feathers with a slightly ineffectual right leg before settling. "I like other folks well enough, but I find most conversations end in people talking at, rather than with, one another and I find that tiring. I think I would welcome the company of brilliant people--you know, Shelley or Wilde---but as far as I am aware they are dead. So, on balance, I prefer to keep mainly to myself."

He fell silent, and so I took out my brushes and began to paint. There was something abstracted and apart about him; and as I worked, looking more closely at the details of his face and bearing, I came to realise that he was quite separate and sufficient in himself.

By early evening, with the sun hanging low and warm in the sky, I finished my painting and we parted ways. I made him promise that he would come and stay with me the minute he felt cold and wet, for I knew the rose bush would offer him little shelter once the weather turned. He promised to do so, yet I felt in my heart he might not. When I finally turned to leave and caught one last look at him, lying there among the roses, so handsome and golden in the dwindling light, I left a little piece of my heart with him.

Chapter Six

The Sisters

The weekend passed, and by the following Tuesday morning, I was beginning to wonder if Connie and Madge would ever visit. Then, in the early afternoon, there was a brisk pecking followed moments later by a long ring of the little bell I had installed at Vernon's request, and I opened the door to find the sisters who were so engaged in an animated conversation that they failed to notice me.

They were wonderful-looking turkeys, tall with caramel brown feathers. Over their wings and backs, they wore shawls of moss green and brown paisley, and standing together, they made a striking sight. I coughed slightly to attract their attention, and as they turned to face me, Connie's neck wattle was lit from behind by the bright afternoon light and shone like pretty pink and yellow glass. I made a quick mental note to include this detail in their portrait; it looked so lovely.

"Well, hello!" said Madge in a loud and commanding voice as she stepped confidently forward. "You must be Jayne? I do hope so; we have walked quite a way to get here, much farther than I had anticipated."

"Yes, I'm Jayne," I replied, smiling, "and you must be Madge and Connie. Please come in."

I stepped to the side so they could enter.

"Don't mind if we do," Madge answered, walking briskly by. "This is Connie, my ever so slightly younger sister, although most people swear we are twins."

Connie followed her sister into the house at a respectful distance, and as she passed, she glanced up, nodded, and smiled warmly like an old friend. "Hello again, Jayne," she whispered.

I showed them both into the studio, where they perched on the sofa's edge.

Madge and Connie in the Hallway

"The wet weather is simply wonderful today," Madge began. "The grey light is sublime; it really shows off the beauty of my feathering." Connie nodded in agreement.

"Would you care for some refreshments?" I asked once they were settled.

"No, not today," Madge snapped a little rudely. "We came here to accept your invitation to be painted. Vernon gave us this note you sent begging to paint us. I understand it will be a golden opportunity for you, and of course, we like doing our share of charity work."

As she spoke, her hawkish eye scanned the room and alighted on the finished portrait of Vernon. "Oh, Vernon! And there he is!" she cried out. "As if in the flesh!" And in one swift movement, she hopped off the sofa and was over by the portrait. "Is it dry?" she asked curtly.

"Yes," I replied, a little taken aback at the speed at which she moved.

She stared at it for some time and was joined by Connie, who demurely hopped off the sofa and quietly joined her sister, standing back a little and looking over her shoulder at the picture from a polite distance.

Madge leaned in, lifted a wing, and tenderly ran a feather around the outline of Vernon's face. "Yes, he is quite the gentleman," she sighed. Connie blinked and looked away, and they stood that way for some minutes as if frozen. "Has Vernon mentioned his feelings for me?" Madge asked, suddenly turning to look me in the eye.

"I know he looked forward to spending time with you both," I replied, not knowing what to say.

"I can well imagine," Madge continued. "He is far too much of a gentleman to declare his intentions outright, but I get the strongest sense he has me in his sights, and I should like it to be known that I would not refuse his advances."

"I know you came here to make an appointment, but if you have a little time, I will be happy to begin sketching you both," I offered. "My morning is quite open."

"Very well then, if you insist," Madge replied haughtily. "I imagine having the opportunity to paint us must be quite an honour so early in your career."

I posed them near the window where Vernon had been painted, with Madge in front and Connie a little to the back and standing to the left, and as soon as they had settled, I began to sketch. It was hard work, as Madge was a fusser and kept changing her posture and directing Connie to do the same. To regain some kind of order, I asked her to tell me everything about the hats that Vernon was making, and instantly, she was beaming.

Madge Boasting

"Well, where do I start?" she began excitedly. "I decided several months ago that with all our important civic duties relating to the church, we needed to have hats made, nothing extravagant, just neat, fitted, something demure. Of course, green is my colour; if you look closely, you will see my eyes are a lovely hazel with quite a lot of green, that's very rare. I asked around and discovered that Vernon makes the finest hats, so we made an appointment. Of course, being so active in the community, I was aware of Vernon. I had seen him on several social occasions but had never been formally introduced. Well, when we arrived for our initial visit and he opened the door to greet us, I was quite taken with him, very handsome...very gentlemanly. I am sure he was being polite in the beginning, but very soon I sensed he had feelings for me that were more than Platonic. He sourced the finest moss green fabric for the hats, and when I suggested a veil, he didn't bat an eye, thought it was a very good idea! I just know that we had many more fittings than is the norm. When I started to drop by with baked goods, he was always cordial and very appreciative. I think his bachelor days may be numbered; we will make the finest couple!"

During Madge's speech, I noticed that as she glowed, so did Connie wither slightly, though I was not sure why. "So, Connie," I asked, "do you like your hat? And did you have as much fun visiting Vernon as your sister? He is such a grand bird."

"I enjoyed my time with him very much," Connie replied politely. "He is masterful at hat making...A real artist; each creation is carefully designed to bring out the individual beauty of the customer."

"Oh yes!" interrupted Madge, almost bursting. "He did mention that MY hat, in particular, was very specially designed to draw attention to my long and elegant neck; I think he was most impressed with it. And the final colour of the fabric was exactly the green of the flecks in my eyes. It's very rare, as I'm sure you know. I can't wait to see it for myself!"

"So you have not seen the finished hats?" I asked.

"No, we don't get to see them until they are sent here," she replied, "I wouldn't be surprised if there wasn't a letter in with mine, something of a sweetheart note."

I couldn't help but feel for Connie. When I had seen her on the path a few days before, she was radiant, and yet here, beside her sister, she had shrunk down to almost nothing, and the glow had been drained right out of her. It seemed so unfair that Madge could have two suitors while she had none, but then, sometimes life seems to be that way, showering plenty on one who seems less worthy.

"Of course..." Madge struck up again, "Of course, should we become betrothed, Connie would be welcome to live with us, not in the house, of course, but very nearby. I took a look in Vernon's garden, and there is room for a nice little building to be erected. I feel that even a spinster can be happy if she is near to her family."

"I don't think there is any reason to imagine that Connie would ever end up a spinster!" I responded, perhaps a little too fiercely. "Besides, that is such a dated term. People can marry or not marry, when and who they will. There should be no stigma to those kinds of choices."

But my comments, if even heard, fell on deaf ears, for Madge, by this time, was in full swing.

"Of course, there is no shame in living without a mate. For some of us, there is that perfect match, while for others," she gestured with her head toward her sister, "a life of service to the community might be a better option. After all, there are only so many suitors to go around." She leaned forward and briefly rubbed her cheek on Vernon's painted face.

Connie, looking deeply crestfallen, did her best to keep her beak held high, and as I finished my sketch, I strained to remember the smiling face I had seen just days before and painted from memory as best I could.

Harder still was painting Madge in any kind of flattering light. I was quite mad at her posturing and showing off, and it stung all the more to think that she had all the romantic cards in her favour. Consequently, my heart was not in it, and her sketched face looked hawkish and cold, so much so that I had to rub out the lines several times and force myself to paint something kinder and less severe, if only for Vernon's sake.

The removal of so much paint left a brown patch on the white canvas, and when it was time to leave, Madge strode over to look at my work and noticed it at once. "I see you have easily captured Connie's simple prettiness," she commented dryly, "but my more exotic beauty must be harder to express by an inexperienced painter such as yourself. I hate to sound nit-picky, but I feel it needs work. I will return tomorrow for another sitting, this time alone. We can see ourselves out. Come along, Connie!" And with that and a quick nod of the head, she was off, poor Connie trailing quietly behind.

Connie

Chapter Seven

The Irritating Guest

The following morning, the rain had gone, and I sat outside enjoying a cup of tea in the warm autumn sun. Far below, a wood fire burned, and the sweet smoke scented the air and lent a misty veil to the golden valley below.

My thoughts drifted up the hill to Quentin. I fancied he would be out, preening himself and enjoying a dust bath under the heady blooms. Everything felt right with the world, and I was beginning to drift off when suddenly I felt eyes upon me.

I looked up from my cup, and there was Madge, standing tall and proud, all sharp angles and eerily pale skin. I cannot say I was happy to see her, but tried my best to be civil.

"Good morning," she began at once. "I trust you are ready for our sitting."

"Sitting... oh yes, I suppose," I replied with all the cheeriness I could muster. "If you stay here, I will bring out the easel. It will be easier and quicker that way, and I know your time is precious."

"I'm in no hurry," she responded. "I enjoyed our conversation yesterday and feel very refreshed. I believe the hats will be here any day now."

I nodded. "If you will excuse me for a moment, Madge," and I went into the house to fetch my supplies and the tea tray.

When I returned, I had her stand to the side as she had the day before and began to sketch in silence. After a few minutes, she began to talk. "Is that Earl Grey?"

"Yes," I replied.

"Oh, I just knew it! Absolutely! I could smell it from here. My father used to drink it. Do you know it's Vernon's favourite kind? Wherever did you get it? I imagine soon I will be buying it myself."

"I found it in the cupboard," I replied, gesturing in the direction of the kitchen.

"Really?" she said, not listening to a word. "Did I mention it was a family favourite? It's quite amazing how everything falls into place, for me especially I think, life, love... it all happens perfectly, just so."

There was a delightful moment of silence. I was sketching quickly, trying desperately to capture her in a flattering light so I could get on with my day.

"I heard you visited the church." she struck up again.

"Yes, it's very charming." I tried to keep my answers short and ask no leading questions but to no avail.

"You may think it's lovely now, but Jayne, you should see it in late spring. On the morning of a wedding festooned with flowers! We do the flowers, you know, Connie and I... well, she helps. I have more of an eye for colour and form. She is good at climbing ladders to hang the swags high, and she takes direction well."

"It sounds as though you make quite the team," I replied, not knowing what else to say. "I am almost finished."

"Oh, do let me look!" she cried and came right over. "As I said, I have the eye." She leaned in close to inspect my sketch. "I have some suggestions now, don't be offended. I know you are the artist, but I can see things not many can see. She peered at the picture, her beak barely an inch from the canvas. "I can be your eye, and you can be my hand. I've never taken the time to learn to use a brush; there are too many important matters to attend to. Now let me see... Yes! Connie looks a little too large; surely she was standing farther back? And I think, in fact, that I need to be painted a little more prominently. Here, pass me the brush, and I will show you."

It was at that moment I almost lost my patience and dearly wanted to ask her to leave but somehow managed to resist.

"No need for that," I assured her, perhaps a little curtly. "I can see what you might be thinking, but remember, there are hats to consider. We don't want to make you so large that your new hat can't be featured on the canvas."

"Ah yes, the hats!" Madge cried out wildly. "Did I tell you about the veil? Vernon thought it a perfect idea. It's being made in France by mice that specialise in such very fine work. Normally, only royalty can afford it, but... well, I thought it worth the stretch."

"That reminds me, I found some lovely antique lace in a cupboard upstairs," I began.

"Lace... yes!" She interrupted, "Did I tell you about the simply beautiful lace kerchief that was given to me by an admirer years ago? Very handsome bird, but a little low brow. I was travelling at the time, full of joie de vivre. I kept the lace and ditched the suitor." She cackled in delight and then kept on talking, and my mind wandered, so I cannot tell you what she said.

I stood there wishing that she would leave, and my thoughts began to drift. She must have noticed because I was suddenly brought back by a sharp change in the pitch of her voice. "Well! I can see I've quite outstayed my welcome!" she snapped. "I must be going anyway—I have more important matters to attend to."

"I'm sorry, Madge. My mind wandered off," I apologised, feigning a yawn.

"I have heard that can happen to artistic types," she replied, and the tone of her voice made the description sound damning. "Never mind! Get back to playing with your paints, dear. I have real work to do." Then she turned on her heel and was gone.

The Finest Tea

Chapter Eight
The Secret

I had a fitful night of sleep. Madge somehow managed to intrude in every dream, twisting my generally happy inner life into a series of frustrating acts centred around her impossible needs, and I felt grateful when the sun finally rose and spared me more of her spectral company.

I needed to confide; I needed to see Quentin, so I quickly got dressed and hurried down to the kitchen. There, I threw together a batch of scones, which I popped into a basket along with a flask of tea and two small cups, then gathered my things and headed straight out of the kitchen door and up the hill towards his home. The hazy orange morning sun painted the landscape in pale colours, and the air held the silent promise of a perfect day.

When I reached the top of the hill, I walked along the

hedgerow until Quentin's bush came into view, and there I saw him, lying out on his side, preening his feathers in the gentle morning light. He looked up, spotted me, and waved a wing in greeting. I waved back and held my basket up in front of me.

"I brought food!" I called as I approached. He nodded and watched until I reached him. "You will need sustenance while I finish painting you," I sat down beside him on the soft dry earth, "and I need your ear. The last few days have really been trying."

"Let me guess. Madge," he replied confidentially, looking into the basket I had placed between us.

"Who else?" I sighed, taking out the scones and unwrapping them, "She's everything you said she would be and more!"

I set a scone before Quentin and poured him a cup of tea. "It's chamomile," I reassured him as he looked at it suspiciously, "it's supposed to calm the nerves."

"Well, you'd better drink up then. You look quite piqued, Miss," he replied.

We sat together and sipped our tea.

"How is your poem coming along?" I asked at length, "You had better hurry with it. I believe Dr. Postlethwait may have some competition for Madge's affections."

Quentin looked at me quizzically. "Please don't tell me it's Vernon," he gasped.

"I'm afraid so," I replied between sips.

"Vernon? What is the bird thinking?...and I always took him to be such a smart fellow." Quentin paused and pecked at his food. "Very nice, and thank you. By the way, I love a good scone."

"It may be the case that they are a poor match in our eyes," I agreed, "but the heart wants what it will."

We both fell into silent thought while we finished eating. When we were done, I shook the crumbs off the blanket, got out my paints and brushes, and began to work on the final details while Quentin sunned himself.

"I'm not sure it could ever work out between Vernon and Madge," he said at length, "there is the matter of his...well, his secret, and I'm not sure Madge could ever approve. Her expectation is always perfection and, of course, strict adherence to ALL social norms..." He looked at me and sighed with resignation. "How well do you know Vernon?"

I was intrigued by his comment. "I don't really know how well I know him, as I'm not sure how much there is to him, but I think he is a fine fellow, and I would love him to be happy in life. I fear the thing he is hiding is holding him back. He did mention something to me. I have no idea what his problem might be, but I know it is bothering him."

"My mother and his aunt are friends, and my mother once told me a story about him," Quentin confided, "Well, I've never told anyone before, but I sense you are fond of him and may be able to help. It's really not such a bad thing and a rather interesting tale."

"Do you mind if I keep painting?" I asked.

"I would like that," he replied happily. "Please, make yourself comfortable, and I will begin.

Vernon was born here, in the barn of your house. His mother, Gladys, was...well, she was a bit of a persnickety bird, wanted everything perfect and always to be the queen of the barn, that sort of thing. His father, Hector, was very similar, tall, handsome, and always needed to be seen as the top rooster, I'm sure you know the type. Anyway, Vernon was the last chick to hatch after his brothers, Oswald and Colin, and his sisters, Verity, Susan, and Agnes. As the chicks hatched, Gladys fussed over and inspected them all. Oswald and Colin were handsome like their father and Verity, Susan, and Agnes were pretty and round with petite feminine beaks and big brown eyes just like their mother, and then..." his voice lowered to a whisper, "and then there was Vernon."

He paused for effect and waited for me to glance up before continuing. "I hear she examined him for a long time, from all angles and in all lights, before finally deciding she had identified the problem. You see, she decided that the top of his head was just a little too round for her taste, and she began to worry about what people would say.

On that very first day, she made a bonnet for him that she tied around his head, and, as he got a little older, she had my aunt make him a fat cap to wear whenever he went outside, with ear flaps and a string that tied under his chin.

The other birds teased him, so he took to making up stories to explain the hats he was forced to wear. The first was that he had to shield his eyes from the sun as they were especially sensitive, and next that he had injured his head. I remember gossip that he was undercover in some kind of investigation and over time the stories became increasingly exciting and impossible to substantiate.

Sometime towards the end of summer, Gladys was sitting with Hector, watching their children play, when Hector mentioned how odd it was that one of his sons always seemed to be wearing a hat. After all, they were a family of straight arrows, and any bending towards bohemian sensibilities would not be tolerated. He called

Vernon over and demanded he remove it and by all accounts, Vernon did just that with not the slightest worry that anything was amiss.

But when he removed his hat, his parents and every other bird in the barn gasped in horror. For you see, being forced to wear hats all his life had caused his ear tufts to grow not straight and stately but curled over like little horns on the sides of his head. It caused quite a scene right there, everyone clucking and laughing at him. Of course, he had no idea what was wrong at first, but when his father shouted at him to 'put on that damned hat and never take it off ' and told him that he was no pheasant and a disgrace to the family."

"Oh that's horrible!" I gasped.

"Yes," agreed Quentin. "Vernon was understandably devastated, just beside himself with shame. He put that hat right back on his head and has never been seen without one since."

"I can't believe it!" I cried, "What a horrid thing to happen."

"And that's not the worst of it," continued Quentin. "When he removed the hat, I heard that Gladys realised that the top of his head was perfectly shaped and that there had been nothing wrong with him in the first place. She knew it was she that had caused the whole fiasco, but she never mentioned so much of a word about it to Hector. It was decided that Vernon was such a disgrace with his 'odd ways' that they cast him out. I don't know how she lives with the guilt, but then again, in my opinion, she doesn't seem right in the head."

"It sounds like a horrible business all around," I sighed. "Poor Vernon."

"Oh, don't feel too sorry for him. He has a wonderful business making hats, and he always looks dashing. In a way, misfortune has made him what he is today."

We sat together musing for a while; the painting was almost done. It didn't have the detail and sharp line of Vernon's portrait but was softer and less defined, like Quentin himself.

"Do you mind if I paint in some of these grasses as a background?" I asked, "I know you're really in front of your bush, but I would love to portray you against the yellows and golds."

"Of course," replied Quentin, "no need to ask, remember you're the artist. Do you mind if I move around?"

"Of course not, please do, I'm done with you," I laughed. "You, Sir, are free to go."

Quentin stood and slowly stretched his legs out behind him, one at a time. "I think, in that case, I am going to finish the poem. It seems its timely arrival might save our friend."

He disappeared into his bush, where there was a faint rummaging sound, and after a few minutes, he reappeared. "I wonder if the muses are with me today?" he asked no one in particular, then dropped a sheet of parchment on the corner of the blanket and sat beside it. There was a flurry of activity, and he produced a small ink bottle, paper, and a quill pen out from under his wing (a feat which I would have liked to have seen in more detail) and began to write.

We sat working side by side until the painting was complete and a bank of high clouds rolled in from the sea, obscuring the sun.

"I'm done!" I finally pronounced, "Would you like to see it? I think I might go soon. It's getting chilly."

Quentin put down his pen, and I turned the painting around to face him.

Quentin Writing

"Well, well, who is that handsome bird?" he asked quizzically, "I think we might need an introduction."

"Quentin, meet Quentin," I replied, laughing as Quentin bowed his head slightly, "so you like it?"

"Like, my dear, what are you talking about? I simply LOVE it!"

"Would you like to keep it?" I asked, pointing toward his rosebush. "It's really quite sturdy, and being oil very resistant to the weather, you could even use it to patch the roof."

"Don't be silly," Quentin replied sternly, "I think it's very good indeed. Take it home to Rookscroft. That way, when I visit, I can feel important, like the lord of the manor." He stuck his beak up high in an affected pose, which honestly quite became him.

"You can pull off that look." I giggled.

"Flattery will get you everywhere," he joked. "Now, I might be wrong, but I have the strongest suspicion it is about to rain, so you might want to gather up your things and head back home...unless you want to brave the thorns with me." He indicated towards his house.

"Thank you for the invitation, but don't think I'd fit." I laughed as I loaded my art supplies back into my bag.

"Hopefully I can get back before it starts. Otherwise I might be using your portrait to stay dry."

"You'd better not," he replied with mock sternness.

I stood, and as I turned to go, I watched him tuck his belongings up under his wing and make his way back to the safety of his home. "Hurry up and get that poem sent to Madge!" I called after him, "Remember, lives are at stake!"

As I made my way down the hill, the sky darkened, and I could see the misty curtain of rain quickly advancing over the mountains towards the house, and I just had time to slip through the kitchen door before the torrent reached me.

Quentin

Chapter Nine

Hats

That afternoon, the hats arrived. There must have been a knock at the door, but I missed it. I was going out to gather some carrots for dinner when I noticed them on the step: two little round hat boxes covered in plum-purple silk, tied with bows. They were small enough to fit in the palm of my hand and so perfect that I wished I could open them and peek inside, an urge that I resisted. Under the bows, I noticed notes. One had Connie and one Madge written in fine calligraphy. I could hardly wait for the next day when I could see the contents inside, and I put them on the mantle for safekeeping.

The following morning, the sisters returned, and despite my feelings from the day before, I found myself hurrying to greet them. "Good morning, ladies, do come in. Your hats are here!" I called excitedly as I opened the door.

We made our way to the studio, where the boxes were waiting on the table. "Would you like tea?" I asked.

"Maybe in a while, dear, I can't wait. I must see my hat," replied Madge, all a dither.

The sisters took seats side by side on the sofa, and I handed them each their little boxes.

"Delightful," whispered Connie, "I have never been given anything like this before." She sat with the box, held in the soft feathers of her wings, quietly admiring it.

"I have a letter!" Madge called out, "Look! Here, tucked under the bow, it is written in Vernon's very own hand!"

"Yes," I replied, smiling. "I believe you both have one."

"Please read it to me, Jayne," Madge requested starchily. "I don't have my spyglass with me, and I need to know every word."

I took the note and sat in a chair facing them both. The envelope was very small and made of fine, cream paper. I turned it over, broke the little red wax seal, and took out the letter. There were two sheets, and I unfolded the first.

"This is an invoice for the hats. Would you like me to read it aloud?" I asked.

"No. No, I can deal with that later. Read the letter to me!" stammered Madge impatiently.

As I watched, she tore the bow open with her beak and clawed off the lid in quite a wild manner, and there, sitting snugly inside, was a small hat made of a glorious moss green with a short white veil around the front.

"It is exquisite!" Madge gasped, "Connie, look at the workmanship, the fabric, THE VEIL! See how it is so perfectly fashioned and the ruching — Vernon quite outdid himself!" Carefully, she lifted the hat from the box with the tips of her wings and held it before her eyes. "Oh my, LOOK!" She twisted the hat around so we could see, and there, on the left side, pinned onto the veil, was a lovely gold brooch with several red stones. "It's a sign!" cried Madge in delight. "Red, the colour of the heart! Just look! LOOK!"

Her eyes were round and huge, her composure entirely gone, and she suddenly stood up on the sofa and held the hat up high in the air. "Look at this magnificent jewel! I'm sure I know what this means! Jayne dear, read the note as I requested and hurry!"

I unfolded the second piece of paper, and indeed, it was a letter.

Dear Madge,

Thank you for allowing me to create this one of a kind hat for you. I very much enjoyed getting to know you and your delightful sister Connie. I have taken the liberty of shortening the veil; after all, this hat is for everyday wear and not for a wedding, and I feel the shorter length is more flattering to your face. I added a little something to the brim. I hope you do not find it garish, just a hint of colour.

Kind regards
Vernon

I finished reading and I looked up to see that Madge was sitting back down, listening to every word for some sign as she carefully eyed her new jewel. I could not read her face; she seemed to be thinking.

"He gave me a brooch... I know this has meaning," she sounded unsure. Madge turned the hat from side to side, looking at the stones as they caught the light. "I think they are rubies..." she finally proclaimed confidently, "Yes, I'm sure they must be! Rubies are the stones of love... did he say vintage? I'm sure he did. Maybe they are a family heirloom? I can't wait to share the good news!"

"Would you like me to help you try it on?" I moved towards her to take the hat.

Her cheeks were glowing as she ceremonially handed it to me. I carefully placed it on her small head and held up a hand mirror so she could see.

She flushed at the sight of herself. "It's perfect, utterly perfect... and the veil — this brooch, of course, is THE finishing touch..." she trailed off, lost in thought.

"You look beautiful, dear sister!" I turned to see Connie — warm and kind-hearted — her little hat box still untouched on her lap.

"You have a note, too," I said, catching her eye and smiling. "Would you like me to read it?"

"Oh, no need for that," she replied quietly, "I can read it myself." She opened the note and appeared to begin reading.

"Jayne!" Madge called out loudly, "I'm going to stand over by the window. Hurry! Mix up some paint and you can begin on my hat! I have little time to spare." I obliged, leaving Connie to read to herself, hoping the more quickly I could get the painting finished, the faster Madge might leave.

Connie sat placidly on the sofa, and glancing over, I noticed that she had put the note aside and taken her hat out of the box. "Would you like to come over here, too?" I asked.

She nodded amiably and joined us.

I helped Connie fix the hat, just so, on top of her head, then she stepped in behind Madge and posed as we had arranged. It took just a short time to paint in the hats, and as soon as I was done, the sisters left, Madge all a spin, promising to return later in the week for their final sitting.

Chapter Ten

A Poem

I was woken by strange noises. It was early morning and as I strained to focus my hazy eyes, I pulled on a robe and headed down the stairs. There was a commotion at the front door and my heart raced as I pulled back the bolt and opened it. To my relief, there standing on the mat was Madge, her eyes ablaze, waving a letter up towards me with her wing.

"Make way," she cried out. "Let me in, do let me in!!! I found this in my mailbox last evening and have been up half the night trying to decipher it." She rushed past me into the studio and laid it out on the coffee table. "I can read 'Postlethwaite' and 'love'. Here, Jayne, read it to me--quickly, I can't wait!"

I took the paper and unfolded it; Quentin had fine penmanship--scratchy, yet elegant. "How exciting, it's a poem."

"Yes, I can tell that much...go on." I read the poem out loud to her.

Since first my weary eyes beheld your face,

and gazed upon your countenance divine.

Since ears first heard the soft croon of your voice,

I dreamed a dream that someday you'd be mine.

Though darling buds may fade in June's hot sun,

this summer has been but a dream to me.

Perchance to spy you on the path, and glance upon,

the beauty everlasting that is thee.

The heart within my breast beats true and bold,

and dreams of days spent in your precious care.

My darling Madge, I hope you feel the same.

One word, and at the church door, I'll be there.

Grenville

I looked up to see Madge before me transfigured, her head slightly fallen and her eyes soft and wet with tears. "I never thought anyone would truly love me," she said simply and fell silent.

"Shall I make us some tea?" I asked kindly. She nodded in reply, and I left her alone while I went to the kitchen.

"I'm not sure what to do," she said quietly, as I returned through the door. I set down the tray and placed her tea in front of her before sitting down. She took a long thoughtful sip. "This, I know, is the real thing. The grand love affair that only comes around once, I have read about them, but hardly dared hope..." her voice trailed off and she stared into her cup. After a pause, she looked up, "Have you seen him?" she asked.

"Not personally, but Quentin has met him and he tells me the Doctor is very fine. A tall, striking bird." I replied.

"All the Postlethwaite's are that way." Madge's eyes were burning with excitement. "A very striking family altogether, not one of them scrawny or dull, I hope I can live up to the name."

"Of course you can! Don't you remember Vernon telling you about your splendid neck?" I reminded her kindly.

"Oh Vernon, he will be crushed." She seemed

genuinely concerned and looked at me directly with her damp eyes.

"Never mind about that, I'm sure he will be fine," I reassured her.

"What shall I do? How do we meet?" Her voice was high and thin.

"Just go to him," I suggested, "right now, I hear he holds a surgery till four..."

"I couldn't possibly, what do I say?" She seemed giddy with excitement and so deeply unsure of herself my heart began to melt.

"You don't need to say anything, just show up. Madge, when someone declares his feelings in this way there is no need for an appointment."

"Go now?" Madge looked down at herself. "Like this? I'm not dressed for it!"

"Put on your new hat and go!" I cried impishly. "Believe me, he will not notice the clothes you are wearing, now drink up quickly so you can be off."

Madge was flushed, she seemed off balance and for the first time since we had met, free and alive. "Oh dear," she cried pausing to look at her reflection in the hallway mirror. "I can't go out like this, all pink and wild."

"Nonsense you look radiant," I replied laughing.

"Do I really? Radiant? Not ruddy like common barnyard fowl?" She turned and looked me in the eye full on, all pretence had dropped away replaced by such frail hope.

"You may be many things, but ruddy and common you are not." I smiled.

Her expression changed and her eyes suddenly burned with excitement. As she turned to go, a flicker of a warm smile played across her face. "Thank you." She said simply as she walked past me and out through the front door. I stood watching as she headed up the lane and trotted gracefully out of sight, her neck slightly forward. Hurrying towards her destiny.

Fall was in the air and the nights were drawing in, the cool evenings drove me inside and I lit a fire in the hearth for the first time. I had heard nothing from my new friends for a few days and was musing that they too must be preparing for the cold winter to come. Then early one cold, foggy morning the little bell at the front door rang and I felt my heart leap as I ran to answer it.

Madge Running

"I have such news!" cried Madge her eyes burning like hot coals "Oh do let us in Jayne, there is such a chill in the air!" she strode past me into the house followed by Connie who as usual smiled in welcome.

"Generally," she began, "I'm in favour of Spring weddings as you know, new beginnings and all that. But Grenville simply cannot wait. So it will be a fall wedding, pumpkins, candles, apples, oh and chrysanthemums and wheat for the table displays...Write that down Connie, don't be slow..."

By now we had reached the far end of the hall where Madge paused to adjust her hat in the mirror.

"I suppose," she continued, "that this old hat should remain in the painting although a new one is in order. Connie!" She turned to address her sister, "oh Connie dear, do find your hat and put it on! Don't dawdle dear, we are in a hurry, so much to get done." She turned and walked into the studio taking her place at the far side of the room next to the window.

"Now let me think, flowers, hymns, a guest list. Oh, the guest list! I must get Grenville's family's details, we can't leave a one of them out. I believe he has cousins in the South. Connie, write that down then hurry over here."

"I'm so excited for you Madge." I finally commented, as I hastily squeezed out paints on the palette.

"Congratulations!"

"Well thank you, I'm sorry for Vernon, of course, truly I am, but the early bird catches the worm and after all a Dr trumps a Hatter every time, don't you think?"

As Madge was speaking Connie walked in behind her and quietly took her place next to her sister. I noticed she wore a lovely pin in her hat with a matching pearl necklace. "What a lovely necklace," I began, "where did you get it?"

Madge, wrongly, assumed I was addressing her, "I'm so pleased you noticed it, yes it IS very lovely," she looked down on her chest at the new pendant she was wearing. "It's a Postlethwaite heirloom, very old, very rare... Passed down for generations from mother to eldest son, to give to his bride..." And so she continued on, in fact, she hardly paused to take a breath. I will not bother you with details, but the conversation dealt with the finer points of her coming nuptials, which I will spare you.

"I think it's done." I finally pronounced standing back from the canvas and tilting my head.

The sisters came over and Madge cast her infamous eye over the painting. "Not bad" she commented "I see myself as I formerly was, single and playing the field... Connie is still the same... Of course, you will want to paint me on my wedding day." I smiled politely, wishing to keep my answer vague.

"Well come along then! We don't have all day. Thank you for the portrait Jayne, I will write and let you know when we would like it to be delivered, in the meantime you may keep it here. In return I would like to invite you to the wedding, you will get a good seat, behind my relatives on my side of the church... In the back." And with that, they were off, Madge with a distracted wedding-crazed air and Connie following some steps behind, a smile playing over her face.

Chapter Eleven

The Answer

My sleep that night was broken by wild whooping and howling that rang out from the forest. At one point, I was jolted awake by a crashing sound below my bedroom window. "They are here," I thought to myself and pulled the covers tight over my head before drifting back to a restless sleep.

I was awoken at daybreak by another noise, this time a dull thud somewhere outside, below my window. I hopped out of bed, wrapped my robe around me and hurried downstairs, fearful of what I might find. With trepidation, I opened the front door and began to walk around the house. The marine layer had returned making the air heavy and grey outside. I was painfully aware that I had no real method of defence and could not yet see clearly as my eyes were struggling to adjust to the light of day. As I rounded the final corner, to my immense relief,

I found the source of the noise, poor Vernon, stuck upside down in a large lavender bush under the studio window, his legs up straight in the air, unable to wriggle himself free.

"Oh, hello!" I called to him. "What happened? Let me help you out."

"Well, nothing much... I...I'm not sure," stammered Vernon. "I was admiring the flowers and must have slipped somehow... " I smiled and hurried over to help him out.

"You smell all fresh and lavendery," I commented as I helped dust him off. "Would you like to come in for breakfast?"

"I believe I would," he replied and followed me into the house. He paused for some moments at the studio door, and I noticed he seemed to be trying to look in.

"The kitchen is this way," I indicated with my hand. "Oh yes," he replied vaguely. "The tea...yes."

Vernon in the Lavendar

I noticed that he seemed distracted and began to worry that perhaps he had hit his head in the fall. "Would you like something to eat? I have a fresh loaf of currant bread, I can toast it if you like."

"Toast...toast..." He seemed to be somewhere else. "Oh, yes, toast. That will be fine." He perched on the edge of a kitchen chair while I cut a slice. "Have you finished the portrait of the sisters yet?" he asked after a moment's hesitation.

"Yes, it's in the studio drying. I was thinking of taking it over later today." I replied, setting the plate in front of him.

"I have to see it!" He cried out and before I could say another word, he jumped down and headed out of the kitchen, toward the studio at great speed. I followed close behind and reached the room to find him, his back to me, staring at the painting.

"I hope I have..." I began, but he turned abruptly.

"I am sorry to cut our visit short," he interrupted all a dither, "but I must go. Right away!"

And without another word, he turned and ran for the door, right past me and off down the driveway, his wings half extended, through the gate and out of sight.

I stood in the studio for some time staring at the turkey sisters painting, trying to look for some sign that might explain his strange behaviour but could see nothing out of place.

Vernon's hasty departure left me feeling a little off balance and try as I might I could not get back to my regular morning routine. I tidied around the house, but when I tried to settle down to paint I found myself restless and without inspiration so I decided to clear my thoughts with a short walk and a visit with Quentin.

As I set out, the sun began to burn through the high gauzy mist and hung like a white spectre over the treeline. I walked quickly up the hill, two slices of currant loaf tucked into my pocket. As I moved further from the safety of my home I felt increasingly alone in a cold unfriendly landscape and my thoughts were plagued by memories of the wild sounds from the night before. I prayed with all my heart that I would arrive at the rosebush and find Quentin safe and warm but as I approached I did not see him sitting out in his usual morning spot and my heart began to sink. I ran over and crouched down low peering anxiously into the dark spiny interior, but there was no sign of my dear friend.

"Quentin!" I called. "Are you home?" but there was no reply. I called again, over and over, but the only sound was the distant calls of hungry crows.

Not knowing what to do, I sat alone by the bush on the soft dirt in silence, waiting. Had some wild creature taken him in the night? Would I ever see my dear friend again? My stomach felt like an empty pit, and suddenly I felt all at sea, lonely and adrift in an uncertain world.

"Is that you?"

My heart leapt up and I turned toward the familiar scratchy voice coming from the unseen depths of the bush. Slowly Quentin emerged all rumpled and golden, his eyes half open. I jumped to my feet and as soon as he was within range, reached forward, grabbed him and held him tight to me, all feathery and soft.

"I thought I had lost you!" I sputtered through tears of joy. "I thought I was alone again."

"You're not that lucky," he replied looking down at my coat. "Is that currant bread in your pocket?"

Laughing, I carefully put him down. He shook out his feathers, and together we sat down in our usual spot. I cannot begin to explain the relief and happiness I felt at finding my wonderful friend all feisty and fine.

With joy, I broke out the bread which we ate in a few minutes of happy silence. The sun was burning through the low gossamer clouds and shone ever more brightly, warming the world with the soft orange glow of an autumn morning. It was as though Quentin himself had brought out the sun.

"How is your day so far?" He asked, breaking the silence. "You always seem to get so much done before anyone else is up."

"Not this morning," I replied. "This has been a very odd and unsettling day until now. Apart from thinking you might be gone, I had a very odd visit from Vernon."

"Do tell! You know I love a good story."

So I proceeded to tell him about Vernon's strange visit. As I did he listened attentively nodding, and when I had finished he looked at me with his round golden eyes, then cocked his head to one side.

"Oh," his voice was soft, "There is no need to worry, I know what happened, just wait here." He scurried off into the bush returning moments later with some rolled up paper which he dropped in my hands.

Quentin and Cake

"Vernon had me write letters to Connie and Madge. He dictated them, of course, since his penmanship leaves a little to be desired, and he wanted everything to be perfect. These notes went with the hats he made for each of them. This is a copy of his letter to Connie. I smudged it at the end, as you can see, so had to rewrite it and, well anyway, I think it will answer your question."

My Dearest Connie,

Please do not think me forward, but my heart compels me to confess my deepest feelings for you.

The mere hope of someday spending time in your presence has filled my days with happiness and vigor for life, which I have never felt before I fear that if I do not state these feelings plainly, my heart will burst! As you read this please know that I am in a small room of my studio, pacing anxiously as I await your reply.

If you feel you might have feelings for me too, then please accept the pin and the necklace that are in the hatbox as tokens of my love, they are family jewels that have been handed down over generations.

I know this letter must come to you as a shock, and I pray it does not embarrass or put you in an uncomfortable position. Therefore, if you accept my advances, please have your portrait painted wearing the jewels. If you feel our friendship should remain platonic, please leave them out of the painting.

You, of course, are welcome to keep them either way. I will visit the picture once it is completed, and there, find your answer.

With all my heart
Vernon

Madge and Connie

About the Author

Jayne Siroshton is an artist and author of whimsical, cozy fiction inspired by nature, folklore, and the quiet magic of everyday life. When she isn't writing or illustrating, she can often be found tending her garden, sipping tea, or spending time with her beloved animal companions.

She lives in a small village in Yorkshire, where she continues to create stories that invite readers into gentle, enchanting worlds.

Visit us at Rookscroft & Company in York, England or online at rookscroft.com for more books, gifts and exclusive content.